LOVE
GROWS
EVERYWHERE

For Paul, a courageous grower of things—B. T.
For Mom and Mike—T. L.

Inspiring | Educating | Creating | Entertaining

Brimming with creative inspiration, how-to projects, and useful information to enrich your everyday life, Quarto Knows is a favourite destination for those pursuing their interests and passions. Visit our site and dig deeper with our books into your area of interest: Quarto Creates, Quarto Cooks, Quarto Homes, Quarto Lives, Quarto Drives, Quarto Explores, Quarto Gifts, or Quarto Kids.

First Published in 2021 by Frances Lincoln Children's Books, an imprint of The Quarto Group.
100 Cummings Center, Suite 265D, Beverly, MA 01915, USA.
T +1 978-282-9590 F +1 078-283-2742 **www.QuartoKnows.com**

A catalog record for this book is available from the Library of Congress.

ISBN 978-0-7112-6422-9

The illustrations were created in acrylic paint.
Set in Bodoni 72

Published by Katie Cotton
Designed by Zoë Tucker
Edited by Hattie Grylls
Production by Dawn Cameron

Manufactured in Guangdong, China TT092021

1 3 5 7 9 10 8 6 4 2

FSC
www.fsc.org

MIX
Paper from
responsible sources
FSC® C016973

LOVE GROWS
EVERYWHERE

Barry Timms

Tisha Lee

Frances Lincoln
First Editions

Love
grows
everywhere . . .

From country farm

to city square.

From desert village, hot and dry,

to mountain home where eagles fly.

Love
grows
any place . . .

HOW to
CARE for
PLANTS

It doesn't need a fancy space.
No matter if the walls are bare,
love only needs our thought and care.

Yes, thought and care
are all love needs
to help it grow,
like tiny seeds,

that might seem
nothing much at first

till up into the light they burst.

Love
will
find a way . . .

to brighten any cloudy day.

A gentle hug, a perfect kiss.

A song to bring back
times you miss.

A moment shared, a helping hand,
when things don't turn out quite as planned.

A funny joke
to bring good
cheer.

A kind word
whispered in
your ear.

Love
grows
on the
street . . .

and reaches out
to those we meet.

A neighbor from across the way.
A friend from school
who'd like to play.

MOVING
TRUCK

But there are others
we might see
who need our
help or charity.

As flowers turn towards the sun,
love's friendly smile greets everyone.

Love
  lifts
    hearts and minds . . .

and comes in
many different kinds.

The kind that grows in peace and shade.

The kind too bright
to ever fade.

There's love so great
it fills the room,

and love that takes
its time to bloom.

But each is
precious from
the start—
a miracle
that melts
the heart.

Love
   may
      hide away . . .

when times are hard
and skies are gray.
When hope seems
nowhere to be found . . .

or buried under
stony ground.

But if we're brave,
perhaps we'll dare . . .

to show how much we really care.

A kind of magic
happens then . . .

and love begins to grow again.

Love
grows
everywhere . . .

Enough for all. A gift to share.
Budding, branching,
leaves unfurled . . .

. . . love will make a brighter world.